Copyright © 2002 by Nord-Süd Verlag AG, Gossau Zürich, Switzerland
First published in France by Éditions Nord-Sud under the title *Stanislas et le grelot*.

English translation copyright © 2002 by North-South Books Inc., New York

First published in the United States, Great Britain, Canada, Australia,
and New Zealand in 2002 by North-South Books, an imprint of
Nord-Süd Verlag AG, Gossau Zürich, Switzerland.

Distributed in the United States by North-South Books Inc., New York.

Library of Congress Cataloging-in-Publication Data is available.
A CIP catalogue record for this book is available from The British Library.
ISBN 0-7358-1708-1 (trade edition) 10 9 8 7 6 5 4 3 2 1
ISBN 0-7358-1709-X (library edition) 10 9 8 7 6 5 4 3 2 1
Printed in Germany

For more information about our books, and the authors and artists
who create them, visit our web site: www.northsouth.com

THE
BRAVEST MOUSE

By Maria Barbero

Translated by Sibylle Kazeroid

NORTH-SOUTH BOOKS
New York / London

Sasha lived in an old house with his whole family—his mother, his grandfather, his cousins, his uncles, and his aunts. He was very happy there until one day . . .

. . . while he was nibbling on a grape, Sasha saw himself for the first time. "Huh? What's that?" exclaimed the little mouse.

His mother had always told him he was the most handsome little mouse in the world, but what was that big black circle around his left eye?

"It's hideous!" he moaned. "Why me? I want to look like everybody else!"

From that moment on, Sasha had just one wish—to get rid of the horrible black circle. And one fine morning, he came up with an idea.

"I'll cover that ugly circle with flour," he said.
No sooner said than done. Sasha quickly smeared flour all over his face, then went on his way, totally white and totally content.

But that evening in his bath the flour washed off, and the black circle reappeared.

Poor Sasha. He was so disappointed.

A few days later something happened that made Sasha forget all about the black circle. All the mice were running around in a panic, babbling excitedly to one another.

"What's going on?" asked Sasha.

His mother told him the awful news—Barnabas was back!

"Barnabas? Who's that?" asked Sasha.

"A terrible cat who has no home," explained his mother. "He's the darling of the local ladies."

"Why?"

"Because in exchange for a few treats, he gets rid of all the mice in their cellars and attics. He disappeared, and we thought he was gone for good. But tonight . . . he returned."

His mother was trembling in fear.

Sasha's grandfather called a meeting of the mice. "We have to do something," he declared.

But what?

"If we could at least get a bell around the cat's neck, we could hear him from far away and have time to hide," said Uncle Benjamin.

"An excellent idea," said Grandfather. "But who will dare get that close to the monster?"

All the mice were silent.

Finally, Sasha spoke up. "I'll try," he said bravely.

"Oh, no you won't," said his mother. "It's much too dangerous."

Soon all Sasha could think about
was the bell for Barnabas.
   One day he was sitting in the
meadow thinking about it when,
suddenly, Barnabas rose out of the
tall grass and pounced!
   Sasha didn't stop running until
he reached the drainpipe.

Barnabas was right behind him! He stuck his head into
the end of the pipe just as Sasha crept out of a tiny hole
at the top and raced off to hide in a wardrobe.

Barnabas was confused. Where had that mouse gone?

All night, Sasha replayed the adventure in his head, and early the next morning he leapt out of bed. He knew how he could get the bell around Barnabas's neck!

He found a small bell and carefully slipped it onto a rubber band. He tied the band tightly, making a snug collar for the cat. Then he put the collar around the opening in the drainpipe.

Every Sunday, the lady of the house gave Barnabas a sardine. So, on Sunday morning, Sasha waited, and as soon as the sardine was in the dish, he grabbed it and hid it in the drainpipe.

Now all he needed to do
was to lure Barnabas to the trap.
Sasha scurried around the lady's feet.
"Eeeeeeeeeeeeeeek! A mouse!" she screamed.
Barnabas took off after the little mouse like
a flash! "You again?" he cried, recognizing
Sasha from the black circle around his eye.
is time you won't get away!"

Quick as lightning, Sasha raced outside and jumped into the drainpipe.

Barnabas jumped in after him, but when he saw the sardine, he forgot all about Sasha. *Ymmm*, he purred, reaching for the sardine.

Sasha dashed out of the little hole at the top of the pipe, slid down, and slipped the collar around the cat's neck.

Sasha had belled the cat!

Try as he might, Barnabas couldn't free himself from the collar, and finally, angry and annoyed, he slunk off, the bell jingling as he went.

"Bravo! Bravo!" cried the mice, who had been watching the scene from a distance. "Long live Sasha, the bravest mouse!"

The mice held a grand celebration that lasted well into the night.

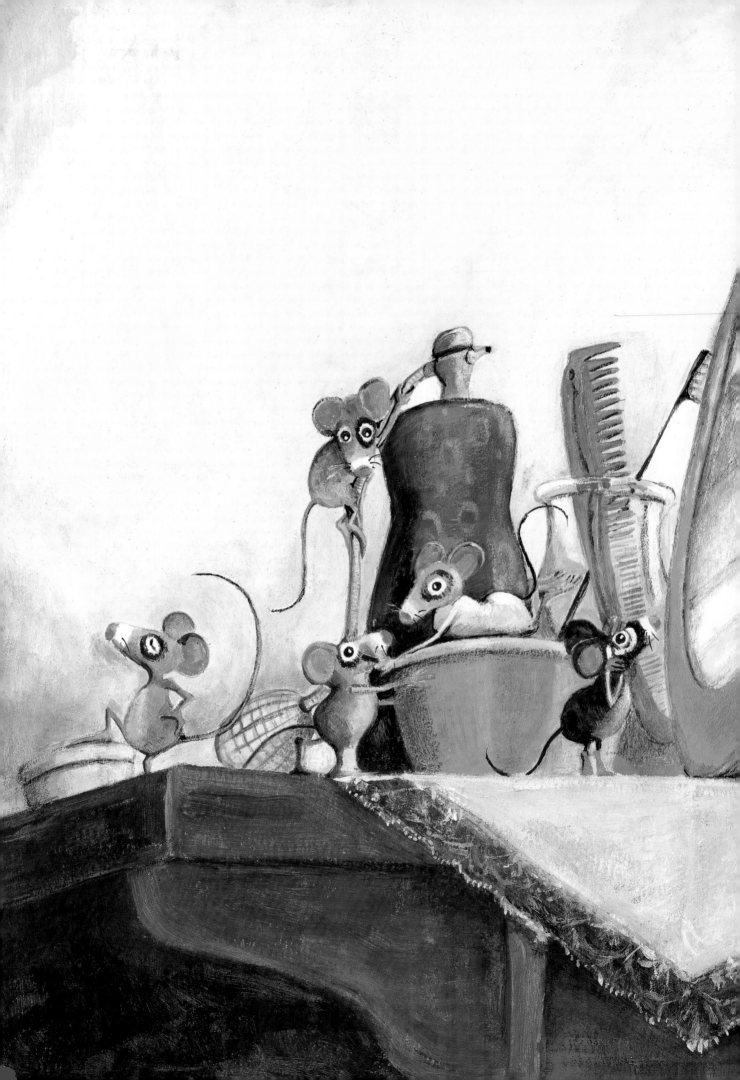

From then on, all the mice admired Sasha. The younger mice even drew big black circles around their eyes so they could look just like their hero.